SHORT TALES
Fairy Tales

Jack
and the
Beanstalk

Adapted by J.J. Hart
Illustrated by Mike Dubisch

WAYLAND

Published in 2014 by Wayland

Copyright © 2014 Wayland

Wayland
338 Euston Road
London NW1 3BH

Wayland Australia
Level 17/207 Kent Street
Sydney, NSW 2000

Adapted Text by J. J. Hart
Illustrations by Mike Dubisch
Colours by Wes Hartman
Edited by Stephanie Hedlund
Interior Layout by Kristen Fitzner Denton and Alyssa Peacock
Book Design and Packaging by Shannon Eric Denton
Cover Design by Alyssa Peacock

Copyright © 2008 by Abdo Consulting Group

A cataloguing record for this title is available at the British Library.
Dewey number: 823.9'2

Printed in China

ISBN: 978 0 7502 7825 6

Wayland is a division of Hachette Children's Books, an Hachette UK company.
www.hachette.co.uk

Jack and his mother had no money and no food.

All they had to sell was their cow, which gave them milk.

'Take her to market' said Jack's mother. 'We need money to buy food to eat.'

So Jack led the cow to the market.

On the way, he met a man.

The man offered to buy Jack's cow.

'I will trade you these five magic beans for her,' said the man. 'They will grow right up to the sky.'

Jack could hardly believe his luck.

But Jack's mother didn't believe in magic beans.

She was very angry. 'You sold our cow for five beans?' she cried.

'Not just any beans, Mother' said Jack. 'Magic beans.'

Jack's mother threw the beans out of the window.

'There are no such things as magic beans, Jack'
said Jack's mother. 'Now we don't have any milk
or any money.'

Jack went to bed without any supper.

In the morning, he found that the man had been right! The beans were magic, after all!

The beanstalks had grown right up through the clouds, higher than Jack could see.

Jack wanted to see how high they went.

He climbed and he climbed and he climbed.

Soon, he could not see his own house.

Above the clouds was a wonderful land.

Jack had never seen anything like it.

He decided to visit the richest, grandest house in sight.

A great big giant woman was sweeping outside the house.

'Good morning' said Jack.

Jack had not had dinner or breakfast, and he was very hungry.

'Have you anything to eat?' Jack asked the woman.

The woman was nice. She invited Jack inside.

Jack was amazed at how big everything in the house was!

The giant's wife gave him bread, milk and a piece of cheese. He sat on the floor to eat.

But soon the whole house began to shake.

It was the giant!

The giant's wife hid Jack inside her oven, just in time.

'Cook these for me, wife!' roared the giant. The giant started to leave the kitchen, but then he stopped and sniffed.

'Fee-fi-fo-fum,

I smell the blood of an Englishman,

Be he alive or be he dead,

I'll grind his bones to make my bread.'

'Nonsense, dear' said the giant's wife. 'Go and wash your hands and I'll make your breakfast.'

She took Jack from the oven and hid him in a cupboard.

There, Jack waited. The giant ate and then sat at the table counting his gold. Soon, he fell asleep.

Jack knew his mother could buy food with the gold. The giant would never miss one bag.

Jack took a bag of gold and ran.

He raced back down the beanstalk.

At the bottom, he showed his mother the gold.

'See, Mother?' said Jack. 'I told you the beans were magic.'

Jack and his mother lived off the gold for months. But one day it ran out.

Jack went back up the beanstalk to see what else he could find.

The giant's wife was outside her house again.

'Please,' said Jack, who was hungry from his long climb. 'May I have some bread?'

The woman was nice and she fed Jack again.

21

Soon, the giant returned.

'Fee-fi-fo-fum,
I smell the blood of an Englishman,
Be he alive or be he dead,
I'll grind his bones to make my bread.'

'Nonsense, dear' said the giant's wife. 'Go and wash, and I'll make your lunch.'

When the giant left, the woman hid Jack in the cupboard.

After his lunch, the giant put a hen on the table. 'Lay' he said. The hen laid an egg of gold.

Jack knew those golden eggs would buy plenty of food!

He waited until the giant had fallen fast asleep.

Then Jack took the hen. He climbed down the beanstalk as fast as he could.

When he arrived home he said 'Those magic beans have given us another treasure. This hen lays golden eggs!'

The hen laid a golden egg every day. Jack and his mother were able to buy all the food they needed.

But Jack wanted to see what other wonders waited at the top of the beanstalk.

A week later, he climbed up again.

He found the giant's wife and she invited him inside. Again he hid in the cupboard.

After the giant ate, a magical golden harp sang a song for him. The giant fell fast asleep.

Jack crept out of hiding to see the harp.

'Master, master!' called the magical harp, as soon as Jack held it.

The giant woke up. Jack was frightened! He ran, still holding the harp.

The giant saw him and gave chase.

Jack hurried down the beanstalk as fast as he could.

'Mother, bring me an axe!' Jack called when he neared the bottom.

She met him with an axe.

Jack gave the beanstalk a mighty chop. It fell over and the giant fell with it.

Safe at home, Jack knew he would never visit the giant's house in the clouds again.

With all their treasures, and each other, Jack and his mother lived happily ever after.